A Note to Parents

Your child is beginning the lifelong adventure of reading! And with the **World of Reading** program, you can be sure that he or she is receiving the encouragement needed to become a confident, independent reader. This program is specially designed to encourage your child to enjoy reading at every level by combining exciting, easy-to-read stories featuring favorite characters with colorful art that brings the magic to life.

The **World of Reading** program is divided into four levels so that children at any stage can enjoy a successful reading experience:

Reader-in-Training
Pre-K–Kindergarten
Picture reading and word repetition for children who are getting ready to read.

Beginner Reader
Pre-K–Grade 1
Simple stories and easy-to-sound-out words for children who are just learning to read.

Junior Reader
Kindergarten–Grade 2
Slightly longer stories and more varied sentences perfect for children who are reading with the help of a parent.

Super Reader
Grade 1–Grade 3
Encourages independent reading with rich story lines and wide vocabulary that's right for children who are reading on their own.

Learning to read is a once-in-a-lifetime adventure, and with **World of Reading**, the journey is just beginning!

Printed in the United States of America
First Edition
1 3 5 7 9 10 8 6 4 2
G658-7729-4-14031
Library of Congress Catalog Card Number: 2012955119
ISBN 978-1-4231-6965-9

For more Disney Press fun, visit www.disneybooks.com

SUSTAINABLE
FORESTRY
INITIATIVE
Certified Chain of Custody
Promoting Sustainable Forestry
www.sfiprogram.org
SFI-01415
The SFI label applies to the text stock

DISNEY

MICKEY & FRIENDS

Huey, Dewey, and Louie's Rainy Day

By Kate Ritchey
Illustrated by the Disney Storybook Art Team
and Loter, Inc.

DISNEY PRESS
New York • Los Angeles

Huey, Dewey, and Louie were excited.
They were planning to
surprise Uncle Donald!

The boys loved to
visit their uncle.
He had a big backyard and
lots of toys to play with.
But their favorite part of visiting
was playing with Donald.

Huey rang the doorbell.
"Hiya, Uncle Donald!" they shouted
when he opened the door.
"Oh, hello, boys," said Donald.
"I was just getting ready
to read the newspaper."

Huey and Dewey
pushed past Donald.
"Did you get any new toys?"
asked Huey.
"What kind of snacks do you have?"
asked Dewey.

Louie grabbed his uncle's arm.
"Come play with us, Uncle Donald,"
he said.
But Donald just wanted
to read his paper.

"Let's go play in the backyard!"
Huey said.
He swung open the back door.
Suddenly . . .

CRASH! BOOM!

Lightning flashed in the windows.
Thunder rumbled through the house.

"Oh, no!" the boys cried.
"We cannot go outside now!
What are we going to do?"

"We could play a game," Dewey said.
"I will be blue!"
"I am red!" said Huey.
"I will be green!" said Louie.
"You can be yellow, Uncle Donald."

The boys played three games.
Dewey won every time.
Donald was <u>not</u> having fun!
"Maybe we should do something else,"
said Huey.

"How about painting?" said Louie.
He found paint and paintbrushes
in the closet.
"You can hang our pictures
on the wall,"
Huey told Donald.

Donald thought painting
was too messy.
"Why don't you boys have
some hot chocolate?" he said.
"I am going to
read the newspaper."

The boys watched the rain
and listened to the thunder.
"There must be something fun
we can do," said Huey.

The boys looked at Donald.

He had fallen asleep in his chair.

"I have a great idea!" Dewey said.

"Let's build a fort."

The brothers gathered sheets,
towels, blankets, and pillows.
They took cushions from the couch
and chairs from the kitchen.

Soon construction began
on the fort!

Huey built a lookout tower
to spy on anyone
outside the fort.

Dewey built a secret entrance.
The boys had to crawl
under two chairs
and over a footstool
to get inside!

Louie was in charge of supplies.
He piled up everything
the boys would need.

Donald was still sleeping.
He did not know that
the boys were building around him.

At last, Fort McDuck was complete!
The main room was big
with lots of space to camp out.
The lookout let the boys
watch for invaders.

The fort's kitchen had
all kinds of snacks.
And the secret entrance was
so well hidden
no one would ever find it!

Suddenly, thunder boomed
through the fort's walls.
"We are being attacked!"
yelled Huey.

Huey, Dewey, and Louie
bravely defended Fort McDuck.
"Hooray!" they yelled.
"The fort is safe!"

All the cheering woke up Donald.
He opened his eyes to find that he
was surrounded by pillows and sheets.
"What is going on?" he asked.

"Do not worry, Uncle Donald,"
said Louie.
"We saved you from the invaders
attacking Fort McDuck!" Dewey added.

"Hey!" said Huey from the lookout.

"The rain has stopped."

"Now can we go play outside?"
Dewey asked Donald.

"I think that is a great idea!"
said Donald.

The boys crawled out of the fort.
They put on their
rain boots and coats.
Donald stayed inside the fort,
where it was quiet.
Now he could read his newspaper.

"Hooray!" shouted Huey, Dewey,
and Louie as they jumped into
the rain puddles.
It was the perfect ending to
their day at Uncle Donald's house!